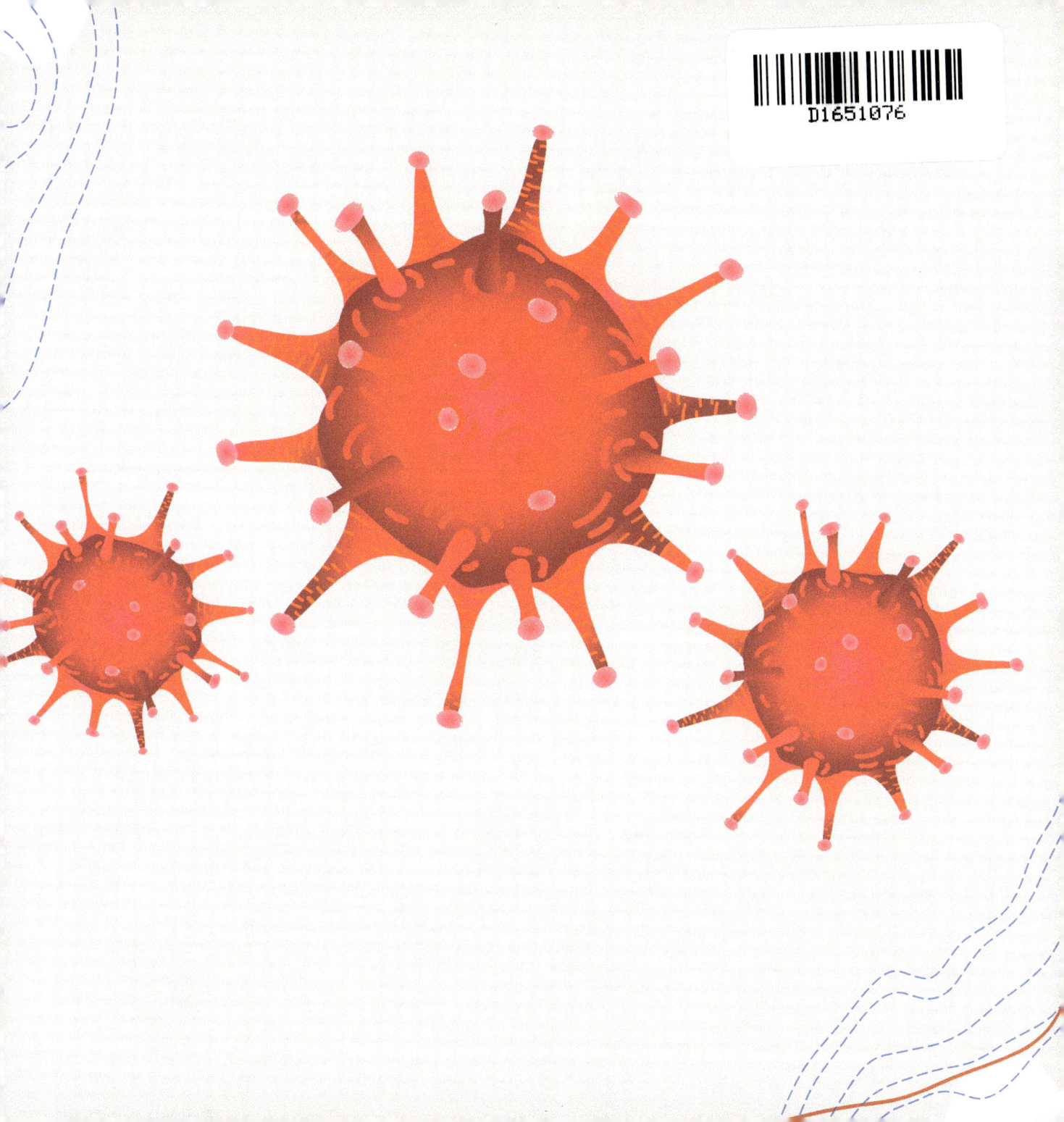

COVID SCHMOVID: A Primer for Survival

Copyright © 2021 by Colleen E. Kelley

All rights reserved.

No part of this book may be reproduced or transmitted in any form or by any means without written permission from the author.

PowerPoint used with permission from Microsoft.

ISBN 978-1-60571-574-2

Printed in USA

ShiresPress (www.northshire.com)

To Nino and to our children

Kita, Elio & Nicholas

with whom we have spent many

happy moments reading together

Covid schmovid, please wear your mask.

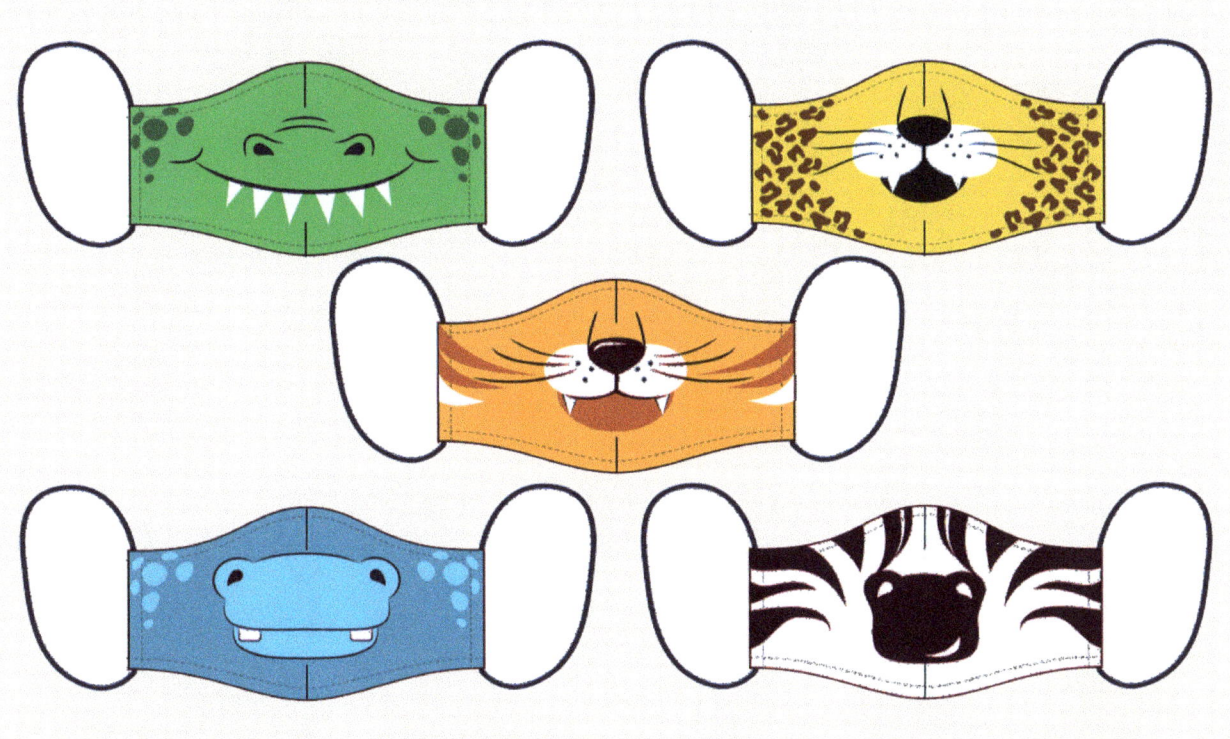

We have plenty

If you need one

of nice ones.

just ask!

**Covid schmovid,
we wash our hands
every day.**

Lots of bubbles

keeps the virus away!

Covid schmovid, please keep your distance.

Three big steps backwards

protects our co-existence.

Covid schmovid, finally there's a vaccine.

It's the best choice we have

to fight what cannot be seen.

Covid schmovid, when will it go away?

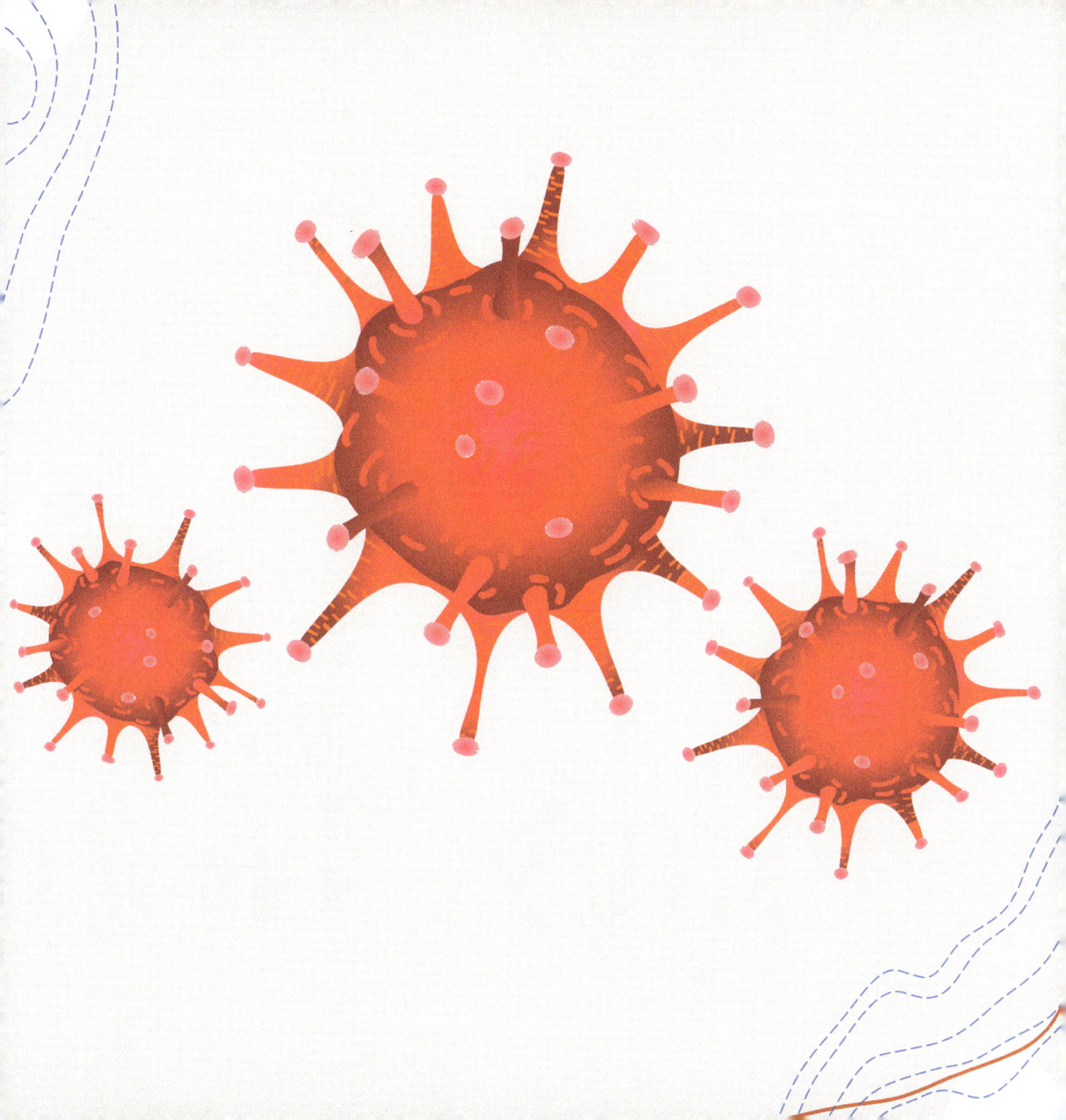

That will likely happen

when we are all ...

very careful every day!

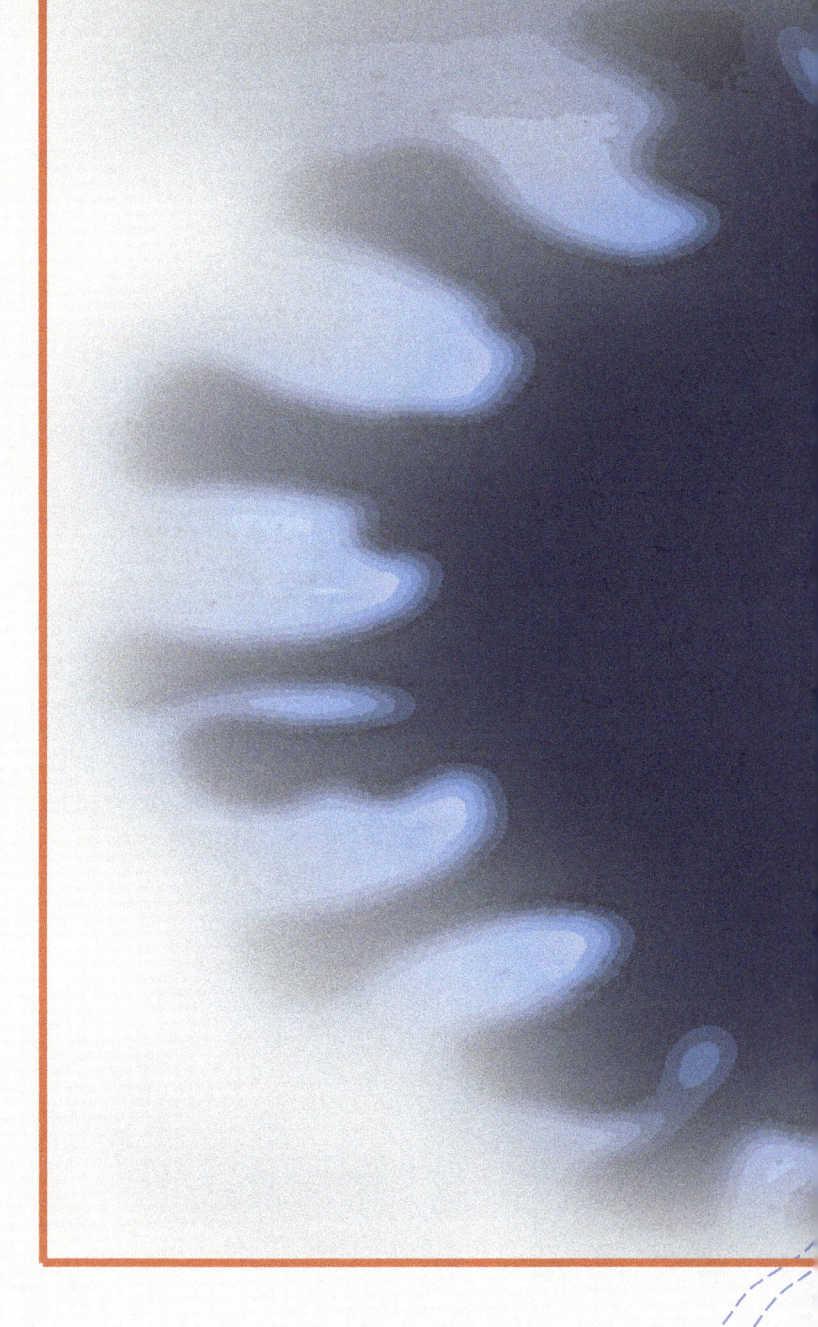

CPSIA information can be obtained
at www.ICGtesting.com
Printed in the USA
BVHW022200060821
613821BV00021B/695